Monsters
The Hunt and the Capture

Transcribed from notes by Bobbi and David Weiss
Illustrated by David Deen

To All Monster Hunters:
You hold in your hands my most treasured possession, my handbook. I am in grave danger. I cannot reveal my name. I am in constant hiding. Too many monsters know of me; too many want me dead.

These pages contain all there is to know of the monsters of the world. You will read of my battles, and you will learn of the monsters' awful powers. You will also learn how to defeat them. If there is one piece of advice I can give, it is to be brave, to always be brave. The monsters greatest weapon is not their strength or weapons or speed; it is your fear. They rely on it; they feed on it.

I have fought all the monsters in these pages at one time or another. Some I have bested, and some have gotten the best of me. If someday one of these abominations should kill me, you will become the keeper of this guide. Use it wisely! Take notes at every turn. There are monsters everywhere! And you, monster hunter, are the only one who can stop them.

Yeti Claw

Frankenstein's Fingernail

Skeleton Finger

Necronomicon Fragment

Mummy Wrapping

Headless Horseman Button

Werewolf Fur

Bigfoot Fur

Yeti Fur

Zombie Viking Hair

Loch Ness Monster's Scale

Silver Bullet

Sand from Mummy's Tomb

Jekyll's Formula

Zombie Brains

Werewolf Claw

Werewolf Tooth

Vampire Fang

Frankenstein's Stitching

Alien Artifact

Alien Uniform

Frankenstein's Monster

This horrifying creature, known only as The Monster, was created by Dr. Victor Frankenstein in the early 1800s. Dr. Frankenstein dug up dead human bodies and sewed his horrifying Monster together like a puzzle, choosing body parts that were not too badly decayed. He brought it to life using lightning. But the Monster's brain was too rotted, and the creature was born insane. It killed its creator, fled, and it now wanders the world, attacking anyone in its path.

AN ATTACK

According to the Bavarian villagers I interviewed, the Monster is almost twice the size of an average man. It also appears to be in constant pain from its mismatched parts. The villagers told me that they had it cornered in a barn, but it actually burst through the back wall to escape. It ran off into the woods and hasn't been seen since.

Sightings

The Monster was created in Germany, but now it roams the globe. It was sighted in 1816 near the Arctic Circle by the writer Mary Shelley.

Capture or Kill?

The Monster is as strong as 10 men, but it is vulnerable to conventional weapons. It is also deathly afraid of fire. But be careful, the mere sight of a flame can send it into a murderous panic.

It must be at least 10 feet tall!

3

Vampires

Vampires are neither alive nor dead but are "undead." This means that although vampires are, by any scientific measure, dead, they act as if they are still alive. Any human can become a vampire if bitten by a vampire or forced to drink vampire blood. Sunlight causes vampires to burst into flame. Because of this, vampires only hunt at night, often with the aid of wolves, rats, and bats. They cast no shadow, cannot be seen in a mirror, and can turn into mist to escape danger.

A FOOL'S ERRAND

I finally cornered Count Dracula! I was armed with garlic, holy water, and a cross. The vampire could not stop me as I loaded a crossbow with a wooden stake. As I took aim, I looked into his eyes. He immediately hypnotized me and escaped.

TOOLS FOR VAMPIRE HUNTING

Crosses

Garlic

Wooden Stakes

Sightings

Count Dracula was first sighted in 1897 by Irish writer Abraham "Bram" Stoker.

Capture or Kill?

Stab a vampire with a wooden stake to pin it down. Then stuff garlic into its mouth and chop off its head. Vampires also hate holy water and crosses. You can use these to force a vampire into sunlight. If you do kill a vampire, make sure you bury its corpse upside-down to prevent it from rising from its grave.

Count Dracula is the King of Vampires. He was once a mighty warrior, Prince Vlad Tepes (TSEH-pesh) of Romania (1431-1476). It is rumored that Count Dracula lives in Romania in his family's castle.

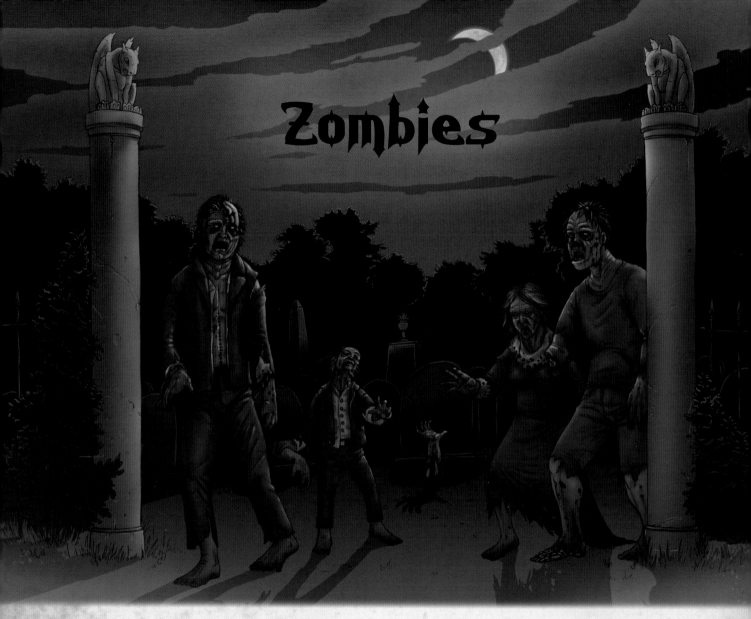

Zombies

Zombies are dead people who have been brought back to life by Voodoo black magic. (Voodoo is a religion involving many spirit powers, and black magic is any sorcery done for evil purposes.) A Bokor (BO-core) is a Voodoo sorcerer who performs rituals to raise zombies. Zombies must obey the Bokor who raised them. Zombies have no special powers, but they feel no pain, which gives them seemingly superhuman strength.

Viking Zombies

Draugr (DROO-gore) are Viking warriors raised from the grave by evil spirits who force them to kill the living. No weapon can stop a draugr. Only the strongest hero can force the draugr back into its grave by wrestling it into the ground and reburying it.

Sightings

Zombies can be found anywhere, usually at night. They can see clearly in the dark.

Capture or Kill?

Make them eat salt. In magical terms, salt is a symbol for earth, which is where a zombie should be—in its grave! Zombies also can be destroyed by burning them and then burying their ashes.

SAVED BY SALT!

As I prowled the city streets in the dead of night, a hand reached from a dark alley and grabbed me by the throat. Zombies move slowly, but they are strong. Once the zombie held me, I could not pull away. It actually tried to eat me! I could hear its Bokor laughing in the darkness. I managed to push salt into its mouth. Instantly, it dissolved into a pile of ash.

Demons

Demons are spirits of pure evil that can take any form they desire. In their natural state, they have wings and can fly anywhere in the universe. They also have the power to summon all sorts of beasts from the underworld.

Demons often try to trick humans into doing evil deeds—from simple theft to waging wars. Powerful sorcerers can summon demons to do their bidding, but demons often attack those who try to control them.

BACK TO THE UNDERWORLD!

A demon almost fooled me by taking the form of my father! But it flashed its red eyes and fangs, which gave it away. After a moment's struggle, I pretended to be hurt and stopped moving. The demon laughed in triumph until I pressed a blessed talisman against its forehead. The demon shrieked, let me go, and disappeared, banished back to the underworld.

Oni

In Japan, demons called Oni (OH-nee) are either pure evil or pure good. Evil Oni cause storms and bring disease. Good Oni protect humans from evil Oni.

Chyernobog

In Russia, Chyernobog (CHUR-no-bog) is a powerful demon whose name means "black god." He brings bad luck and makes people do evil things—lie, steal, and even murder their own families—just for his amusement.

Sightings

Demons like the dark. They tend to live in isolated places, such as graveyards, ruins, and deep in the wilderness.

Capture or Kill?

Demons are spirits, and spirits are eternal. They cannot die. If a demon's body is destroyed, it can simply reappear in a new body. Special amulets and talismans can keep demons away, and people can make the sign of the "evil eye" to make demons flee. But only the most powerful white magic (good spells) can banish demons back to the underworld.

Evil eye sign

Sightings

Mr. Hyde was last sighted by British novelist Robert L. Stevenson in 1886. Concerned for public safety, Stevenson wrote a book telling the world what happened to Dr. Jekyll.

Capture or Kill?

Mr. Hyde is probably somewhere in England. He has no special powers, but his madness gives him great strength.

Dr. Jekyll and Mr. Hyde

A NARROW ESCAPE
I tracked down Mr. Hyde in the English countryside and shot him with a dart containing a madness-curing formula. I do not know if it worked. As soon as he realized I shot him, he attacked me, leaving me bloody, unconscious, and with no idea where he went.

In the late 1800s, Dr. Henry Jekyll wanted to understand the nature of good and evil. To do so he created a potion that allowed him to transform from good Dr. Jekyll to evil Mr. Hyde. Before the potion wore off, Hyde took control of the formula—and the body. Mr. Hyde is still at large and presumably still quite insane.

The Headless Horseman

The Headless Horseman is the ghost of a soldier who fought in America's Revolutionary War (1775-1783). He was killed near Sleepy Hollow, New York when a cannon ball took off his head. Now he rides those woods at night looking for his lost head, attacking anyone in his way.

Sightings

The frightening tale of the Headless Horseman was first documented in 1819 by American author Washington Irving in *The Legend of Sleepy Hollow*.

Capture or Kill?

The only way to stop the Horseman is to find his head and return it to him during one of his nightly rides. But no one knows where his head is! Be warned— even without a head he is still a master swordsman.

STILL ALIVE, BARELY
I offered the Horseman a human skull, but he knew I was trying to fool him. His phantom horse galloped after me so fast that I had to leap off my own steed to dodge his sword! I sneaked back to Sleepy Hollow, filthy and shaken but still alive.

Cthulhu

The main authority on Cthulhu was American writer H. P. Lovecraft (1890-1937), who told the story of the Great Old Ones and the tragic fates that befell those who have tried to find Cthulhu.

Capture or Kill?

The *Necronomicon*, (NEK-ruh-nom-ah-kahn) a long lost book of evil magic, contains spells to rid Earth of Cthulhu forever.

MY NIGHTMARE
Cthulhu spoke to me in a nightmare last night, commanding me to go out and kill in his name. I sought help from Cthulhu scholars at the famed Miskatonic (MISH-kah-toh-nik) University. They cast an ancient white magic spell to protect my dreams.

Cthulhu (kuh-THOO-loo) is one of the Great Old Ones, a race of beings who came to Earth from space. They built their evil city of R'lyeh (RAH-lay) here and dominated the world for hundreds of years before humans took over. Then they decided to rest and allow humanity to thrive . . . for a time. So they sank R'lyeh into the sea. This is where Cthulhu still sleeps, dreaming about the day when the Great Old Ones will rise again and destroy humanity.

Rakshasas

Ravana (rah-VAH-nuh) is the leader of all Rakshasas. He has 10 heads and 20 hands and cannot be killed by gods or other heavenly spirits.

Capture or Kill?

Only the most powerful Hindu gods can defeat a Rakshasa.

Rakshasas (rock-SHA-suz) are the spirits of dead people who were evil in life. They haunt India, appearing in different shapes to torment the living, eating people when it suits them. Rakshasas come in many forms: Pischcas suck the blood of the living, Bhutas can raise the dead, and Grahas spread disease.

THE POWER OF PRAYER
An entire town in India was cursed with a terrible disease from a Graha. Prayer drove the spirit away, and I helped transport the poor victims to the hospital in time to save most of them.

13

A mummy revived using electricity must be destroyed by fire. If magic is used to revive a mummy, then the mummy can only be stopped by reversing the spell.

Mummies

To preserve bodies after death, ancient cultures mummified corpses by using special fluids and cloth wrappings. With the right knowledge, these corpses can be brought back to life. Cheops (CHEE-ops), an ancient Egyptian pharaoh (FARE-oh), was brought back to life in the early 1800s with electricity. The mummy of Imhotep (im-HO-tep), an Egyptian priest, was brought back to life in 1932 with magical tea.

OFF GUARD

After many months, I finally tracked down the museum guard from this famous scene. His nerves were still shaken from his run-in with the mummy. He didn't make much sense, but when I asked what he thought caused the mummy to come to life, he told me, "The storm! The storm!". A quick check at the local library confirmed it: That night there had been a horrible electrical storm.

Skeletons

Some skeletons are raised from their graves by demons who want to attack the living. Other skeletons walk the Earth because the dead person's spirit refuses to leave what's left of their body.

Capture or Kill?

Skeletons tend to be fragile and often can be destroyed by a direct blow, so they attack in large numbers, aiming to overwhelm their victims. One exception is the Baykok. Chippewa Indian warriors told of Baykoks attacking using invisible arrows.

The Grim Reaper

The Grim Reaper comes to everyone when it is time to die. He does not speak, and the air around him is as cold as ice. Doing good deeds is the only way to ward him off.

Capture or Kill?

The Grim Reaper cannot be killed as he is death itself. Once you are in his presence, there is no escape. To amuse himself, he may offer to play a game for your soul. He may even let you choose the game. But be warned: death never loses, and he may treat your soul harshly if the score is close.

15

The Werewolf

A werewolf is a person who changes into a human-wolf form whenever there is a full moon. This curse is called *lycanthropy* (lie-CAN-thro-pee). Anyone bitten by a werewolf becomes cursed. When the sun rises, the werewolf changes back to human form and often cannot remember the horrible deeds done while in werewolf form.

OUT OF TIME

Wearing wolfsbane for defense, I tracked a werewolf for days. But as I reached for my weapon, it turned, saw me, and was on top of me in a single leap! I didn't have time to load my silver bullets. The creature howled when it sensed the wolfsbane and ran off into the dark woods without harming me.

Capture or Kill?

Werewolves can only be destroyed if they are shot with a silver bullet. Wolfsbane (scientific name *Arnica*) is an herb that keeps werewolves away.

EUROPE

faoladh
(FAY-lud)
Ireland

vourdalak
(vore-DAH-lak)
Russia

lobisomem
(loe-BEE-so-mem)
Portugal

loup-garou
(LOOP gah-roo)
France

hombre lobo
(OME-bray LOE-boh)
Spain

Werewolves Are Everywhere!

Werewolves have been found around the globe. Almost every language has its own word for *werewolf*.

Sightings

Baba Yaga uses a mortar and pestle to grind the herbs for her potions. She also flies in a giant mortar, using a pestle to steer and sweeping away her tracks with her broom.

Capture or Kill?

Baba Yaga hides deep in the forests of Russia. She changes location every few days so that no one can find her.

A RESCUE

I just saved a child from Baba Yaga! I had to get close enough to grab the child from her. She cast a spell that badly burned my arm. Still, I feel triumphant! The child is safe, and my burn will heal in time.

Baba Yaga

Baba Yaga (BAH-buh YAH-guh) is an evil witch who eats children. Her hut walks on giant chicken legs and is surrounded by a fence made of human bones. Only magic can stop Baba Yaga, but so far she has always escaped even the most powerful spells.

Faust

Faust (FOWST) was a German alchemist so hungry for knowledge and power that he summoned the devil to help him. The devil agreed to help in exchange for Faust's soul. But when it came time for Faust to give up his soul, he tricked the devil and escaped.

A MONSTER TO FEAR

To me, Faust is the most frightening of monsters. Even if he is little more than an evil man, his intelligence coupled with his capacity for deception make him terrifying. I also wonder if the devil were to offer me such a bargain—my soul for anything in the world—would I take it? I think not, but I have no doubt I would be tempted.

Sightings

Faust was first spotted in 1587. He went by the name Doctor Johann Faustus. German writer Johann Wolfgang von Goethe recorded the most complete account of Faust's evil career in the early 1800s.

Capture or Kill?

Beware! If Faust knows you're looking for him, he will use his evil magic to send demons after you! And no matter what he says, do not trust him. He will do anything to avoid capture.

Bigfoot

Bigfoot are large, shaggy, ape-like creatures that roam the forests of North America. Although they are incredibly strong and violent when confronted, they are not always dangerous. In 1924, Canadian lumberjack Albert Ostman said he had been captured by a family of Bigfoot. They took care of him for a week before letting him go.

Sightings

In 1924, five miners were attacked by several bigfoot in Alberta, Canada. The creatures hurled rocks at the miner's cabin, pinning them inside for days. When the attacks ended, the only evidence was a trail of huge human-like footprints left in the snow.

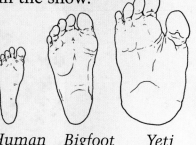

Human   Bigfoot   Yeti

Capture or Kill?

Use tranquilizer darts and hope they penetrate the Bigfoot's thick fur, then capture the Bigfoot in a strong net. Note, however, that their sharp teeth may be able to chew through most standard netting.

CAPTURED, BRIEFLY

Hunting Bigfoot in the Canadian tundra, I got caught in a snowstorm. The temperatures dropped well below zero, and by nightfall, I was lost and snow-blind. At some point, I collapsed. I awoke in a cave. In the corner sat Bigfoot. Foolishly, I reached for my gun. When he stepped forward, I fired at him. He roared at me and ran off. I waited for a week for his return, but he never came back.

This is a terrible picture of the beast. He looks more like this.

SUCCESS (OF SORTS)

After a day-long battle, I managed to kill a Yeti. I'd hoped to capture it, but it broke through my nettings and shook off my tranquilizers. I had no choice. Unfortunately, he weighs as much as five men. Given the freezing temperatures and my lack of transport, I had to leave his body behind. He surely will be devoured by the time I return (if I even can return). With nothing but a tuft of fur for evidence, will anyone believe me?

Yeti

Like Bigfoot, Yeti (YEH-tee) are big and shaggy-haired, but their fur is white and their tracks are bigger. Also called the Abominable Snowmen, the Yeti haunt the Himalayan Mountains which border India, Nepal, and China. Some scientists think that Yeti and Bigfoot are related.

Sightings

In 1938, Captain d'Auvergue, curator of the Victoria Museum in Calcutta, India, almost died of cold while traveling in the Himalayas. He was rescued by the Yeti, who nursed him back to health.

Other Ape-Like Creatures

Taku he (TAH-koo HAY)
Sioux Indians

Sasquatch (SAZ-kwach)
Canada

Yowie (YOW-ee)
Australia

Hibagon (hee-BAH-gone)
Japan

Yeren (YEH-run)
China

Sightings

No one knows what Nessie's whole body looks like. There have been almost 100 sightings recorded, the first in 1871. Most reports say she is as long as 45 feet, has several humps, and is shaped like an eel with four paddle-like fins.

The Loch Ness Monster

This mysterious monster lives in Loch Ness (LOCK NESS) (Loch is the Scottish word for lake). Scientists have used sonar equipment to locate "Nessie" underwater, but no contact has been made. The monster surfaces now and then, but it seems to want to remain hidden. Some suspect she may be the last surviving dinosaur.

INTO THE LOCH

Armed with sonar equipment and a stroboscopic camera, I rowed out to the middle of Loch Ness, hoping to spot the monster. Instead, it spotted me! It flipped my boat over and dumped me in the freezing water! I scrambled back to land without ever seeing the creature, my camera broken beyond repair.

I have finally rid Carter Mansion of the ghost of a woman murdered in a nearby park. I entered the abandoned mansion and spoke to the ghost, who immediately tried to kill me by dropping a bookcase on my head. I dodged it in time and quickly told the ghost that I had found her killer. I heard her whisper, "Thank you," and she hasn't been seen since.

Ghosts

Ghosts are the spirits of dead people who remain on Earth. Apparitions (AP-uh-rish-suns) are ghosts that can pass through solid objects but cannot move them. Poltergeists (POLE-ter-giests) can move objects, make noises, and even hurt people.

Yurei

In Japan, ghosts called yurei (yoo-REH-ee) haunt the living. Yurei are souls of people who were not purified before burial or who died in anger or fear. Some yurei are frightening, some are playful, some are protective, and some are just plain annoying.

Capture or Kill?

The only way to get rid of a ghost is to find out what it wants and help it meet that need. Only then will it leave.

Sightings

In 1947, a spaceship crashed near Roswell, New Mexico. Witnesses saw government officials take alien bodies from the ship. Area 51, a military base in Nevada, is believed to contain these and other alien bodies and ships, although the U.S. government denies this.

Capture or Kill?

H. G. Wells documented the last full-scale alien invasion attempt. In 1898, aliens landed near London, England. They probably would have taken over the world if it hadn't been for a simple germ. Aliens had no immunity to diseases, and the common cold killed them!

Flying saucers zoom at incredible speeds, dive, twist in the air, and hover.

CLOSE ENCOUNTER!
Posing as a scientist, I managed to sneak into Area 51. Yes, alien bodies are there, and I saw a flying saucer with my own eyes! There clearly is life outside of Earth—and it doesn't look friendly.

Aliens

Creatures from space have been studying humanity for decades. They have been known to abduct people and take them to their ships. Most abductees have been safely returned and claim that the aliens were curious but friendly, but some have been taken and never seen again.